by R M Price-Mohr

The egg

weebee book 9a

Published by Crossbridge Books
Worcester

ISBN 978-1-913946-37-1

British Library Cataloguing Publication Data

A catalogue record for this book is available
from the British Library

The weebees

Grog   Pip   Tod   Mop

Jig   Zon   Flup   Saff

The yellow sun is shining in the sky.

Grog is very hot.

Pip has come to play.

She is hot as well.

They are going to jump in the lake to cool down.

Grog has found an egg in the bulrushes.

Pip is excited to find the egg.

The egg is small and smooth.

It has round red spots.

The egg is breaking.

What is going to hatch out
of the egg?

It is a very little dragon.

It is tiny.

It is as small as Pip.

The dragon wants to swim in the lake.

They all go for a swim to cool down.

Flup is flying in the sky.

He can see the tiny dragon in the lake.

The dragon is upset.

He does not have a nest.

The **weebees** are going to help find a comfy nest.

Flup is calling for Tod.
Tod can help look for a
comfy nest.

They go to the oak tree.

They will go down the tunnel under the roots.

In the tunnel they see a ladybird, an ant and a spider.

Grog has found an old
wooden box for a nest.

The dragon is happy to stay with Grog in the old oak tree.